Sacred
Numbers

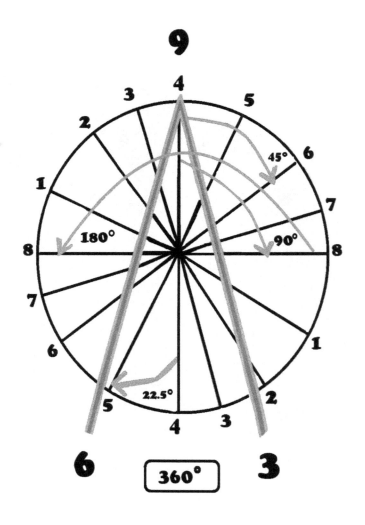

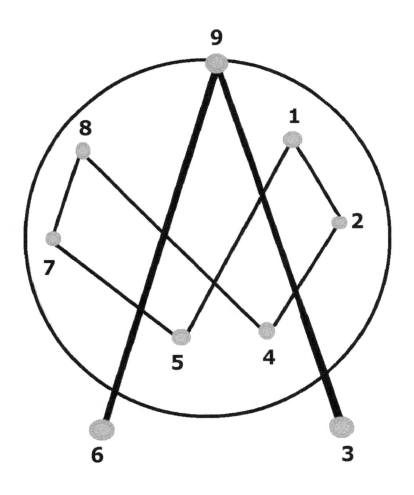

CONTENTS

A Note on "Sacred Number"

Both words and numbers are sacred. Numerical symbols are more than mathematical problems or a way to communicate but perfectly designed to 1.) remind human beings that they are connected to the universe, 2.) serves as guides to find answers in life on earth and 3.) guides to reach enlightenment.

NUMBERS

an arithmetical value, expressed by a word, symbol, or figure, representing a particular quantity and used in counting and making calculations and for showing order in a series or for identification.
https://www.google.com/search?q=numbers+defintion&oq=numbers+de fintion&aqs=chrome..69i57.7451j0j7&sourceid=chrome&ie=UTF-8

<u>Hebrew system</u> letters = numbers = words for dates. Even hieroglyphics contain both numbers and letters to convey messages. In order to connect the relationship between numbers and letters a person has to have principles.

PRINCIPLES

*a fundamental truth or proposition that serves as the foundation for a system of belief or behavior or for a chain of reasoning. *

https://www.google.com/search?ei=h9rnW86wKazG5gKRv63gBQ&q=principals+defintion&oq=principals+defintion&gs_l=psy-ab.3..0i7i10i30l2j0i13j0i7i10i30l7.2234895.2238319..2238692...0.0..4.1176.7479.2j1j4-1j2j3j3......0....1..gws-wiz.......0i71.SlwfGFKl5t4

A fundamental source or basis of something is necessary to even conceive of the possibility of an interrelation of numbers and the universe. Further, understanding how the misuse of words and/or numbers are contrary to the greater good is essential.

ALPHABET – WORDS
MAGICAL SPELLS – VIBRATIONS, ENERGY

Are their power in words? The possibly that you can speak something into existence is shared by many religious faiths. Wikipedia described "magical words" or "words of power" as "words which have a specific, and sometimes unintended, effect." But then proclaims that magical words are often **nonsense** phrases used in **fantasy** fiction." But to the contrary words are more powerful than the spoken word can convey.
https://en.wikipedia.org/wiki/Magic_word

Examples of magical words include "Abracadabra," "Alakazam," "Hocus Pocus," and "Presto-Changeo." (probably intended to suggest 'quick-change').

ABRACADABRA

* is an incantation used as a magical word in stage magic tricks, and historically was believed to have healing affect.

"Abracadabra" may have its origin in the Aramaic language, but numerous conflicting folk etymologies are associated with it. In Hebrew, it translates to "It came to pass as it was spoken."

*Aramaic phrase avra kehdabra, meaning "I will create as I speak" and/or "it will be created in my words." The source is three Hebrew words, ab (father), ben (son), and ruach acadosch (holy spirit). It is from the Chaldean abbada ke dabra, meaning "perish like the word". *

The word abracadabra exhibits patterns. I was able to decode the lottery by studying the numbers and discovering patterns.

ABRACADABRA
ABRACADABR
ABRACADAB
ABRACADA
ABRACAD
ABRACA
ABRAC
ABRA
ABR
AB
A

In decoding the lottery understanding numbers, the purpose of them and the connection between numbers and the universe is necessary. Further, the connection between the universe in understanding the importance of mastering other areas like astrology, medical science, religious concepts, and deities are crucial.

In October of 2018, after predicting the Mega Millions winning numbers 01-28-61-62-63 ball 5 and Powerball 08-12-13-19-27 ball 4 winning numbers days apart, it was clear the numbers released during lottery draws were not random.

I note clear because it was already known to me since I was a child that winning lottery numbers had predictable patterns that allow you to predict winning numbers. This was not the first time in my life that I was able to predict lottery numbers. In my 20's I first predicted three of the five numbers and then the exact numbers for either the Powerball or Mega Millions lottery.

I do not recall the actual name of the draw but it was either the Powerball or Mega Millions. I believe it was the Powerball. Then next I predicted the numbers perfectly but not the ball.

I did not play the numbers at that time because I was taught that gambling was wrong. I did not think that guessing the numbers was anything special or different because I had family members who won the lottery often playing the pick 3 and pick 4.

When I was in college I disregarded what I was taught about gambling because I wanted a few dollars to go to the movies. I played the pick 3. I did not win the draws in straight order but boxed which meant that numbers were out of order but you still get a much smaller prize. Out of order means the number released could be 903 but if you played 930 you still won a prize.

When I was younger I did not think that I had a special ability but it did scare me a little. It was obvious that something was going on despite me merely being able to predict numbers. Being older and doing this again in October of 2018, this ability was amazing to me.

I began a spiritual journey that led me to discover and understand alchemy, prima material, the true meaning of the holy trinity, the connection of the body, soul, and sprit, astrology, mathematics in a new light, and computer science – all without formal educational training. I learned for the first time who Mercury is; a messenger who traveled to earth and how the mind operates.

But the greatest discovery was learning that numbers like letters are sacred. We are all connected to the universe and the higher power uses numbers to communicate with us.
　　　—Melodie Shuler

Part 1

The Meaning of Life

The Reason of Enlightenment – Your Best Self

1.) Know thyself – thy purpose, master thy numbers, master thy senses
2.) Know true love, give true love, show true love
3.) Recognize patters changes and curves
4.) Sacred order of numbers **0, 1, 2, 3, 4, 5, 6, 7, 8, 9**
5.) Basic building blocks to predict lottery numbers are **12, 34, 44, 57, 61 (18)**

The basic building blocks of numbers are based on a base ten number system. The lottery system operators uses both standard algorithms and numerology as an algorithm base. The Mega Millions and Powerball numbers are not double digits but single digit numbers.

The January 1, 2019, winning jackpot numbers were 34-44-57-62-70 ball 14. The number meaning is representative of single blocks. In the January 1, 2019 draw the first number is 3 then next is 4. It is not thirty-four. The graph below shows that the Powerball and Mega Millions lotteries are counted in numerical order with the exception of 576.

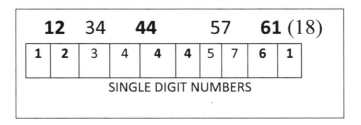

After seeing the patterns in the October 23, 2018 draw and realizing I was catching on to something I started to study previous lottery draws. In two days and two nights, I studied numbers released for both the Powerball and Mega Millions Lottery from November of 2008 to October of 2018. I also believed that the lottery officials were using some type of mathematical formulas so I wrote numbers over and over again and found patterns. Those patterns displayed a 3x3x3 system, 3, 6 and 9 patterns, and algorithms which I later discovered are standard algorithms and a binary numeral system, which uses the base-2 numeral system as a positional rotation with a radix of 2.

I later started to discover that somehow the universe connects us to predict numbers based on astrology because my children could randomly pick numbers that would come out. After I started to teach them numerology they would pick numbers but they would be out of order. Numbers are also used by the higher power to direct us in life. They also direct us to move forward through phrases of life.

Phases of life

Phase 1 Phase 2 Phase 3 Phase 4   Phase 5

01	18	3|6	45	63 (3)

In reviewing the past lottery draws I discovered a repeat of numbers 3,9,6 then 1, 2, 4, 8, 7, 5. I began to use a circle with numbers to predict the lottery with 9 with 3 6 connected. 3 and 6 at the bottom with 5 and O at the center. I call the numbered circle the "Circle of Life."

This information, new to me, seemed so odd that I started to research the information. I researched the use of 3,6,9 to predict lottery numbers. But what I discovered was completely beyond any prior beliefs I had.

I discovered Nicolas Tesla's theories which are also similar to the 5th dimension in the movie "A Wrinkle In Time." Tesla believed there is a third separate dimension and also a 4th higher power (vortex at 5).

It was a game changer when I discovered the seed number to count the algorithm was the last number in order of draw, not the last numerical order. I then created the mnemonic device to help me count faster

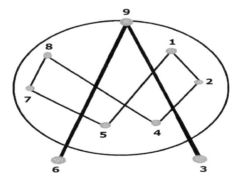

The lottery system operators uses the vortex theory at 5, as a standing still point with 0 also being next to the number 5 = 5/0. Therefore, in following the circle of life the numbers.

predicted can be either 3 then 5 for 35 or 3 then 0 for 30. You have to look at the prior patters to know the correct use. However, 5 is rarely used as the second number and 0 is even rarer but it is possible.

In November of 2018, I wanted to win the lottery on my son's birthday. A few days before his birthday I had a dream about the numbers (1333) (3,9,6) (6,9,3) (9339). I asked my son to write the numbers down. On November 16, 2018, one day after I dreamed those number 33-36-63-68-69 ball 16 were drawn in the Mega Millions lottery.

From my research I later discovered that the Virginia State Lottery Commission used three different algorithms in the Pick 4 and Pick 3 lotteries. They also use the same numerological patterns used by the Powerball and Mega Millions in the Cash 5, and Bank a Millions lotteries. So you can use the same patterns to predict those lotteries.

Part 2

The Lottery Officials Fraud

On October 23, 2018, I participated in an office lottery pool. I was asked numerous times to participate before but I decided to participate this time for some unknown reason. I received a copy of several computer generated sheets. I reviewed the numbers from prior drawings and the computer generated sheets. I picked numbers I thought were consistent with prior patterns.

I did not pick the exact number released for the Mega Millions or win anything but I did catch on to a pattern. The numbers released were 5-28-62-65-70 5.t I believed the first number and the ball would be the same and odd and that two of the prior numbers used in the prior draw would be repeat.

The closest I got was 9 12 41 65 70 9. The last two numbers I picked matched. The last two numbers were also the last two numbers in a prior drawing. The numbers 65 and 70 repeated and I played an odd ball of 9 instead of 5.

Many people claim that the numbers I picked does not mean I was catching on. However, it is rear that any person picks the same first number and the Mega Ball. Further, I got the numbers from the lottery officials own patterns on the computer generated sheets easy picks tickets dated October 23, 2018.

Most importantly, if I had more money to spend, I would have picked other combinations and know for sure that 5 in the beginning and 5 as the Power Ball would have been the beginning and ending of the numbers I would have picked 5 for at least one of those combinations.

Also, the numbers I played 7 12 20 25 32 04 derived from the
easy pick for the Mega Millions draw dated October 23, 2018; 8 11 15 23 57. I intended to play the exact number that was released on October 27, 2018, 8 12 13 19 27 4 but did not. Of course, when I saw the numbers I was little upset that I did not play but at that time I believed

that I did it so many times before I would simply do it again.

On October 26, 2018, I predicting 1 28 61 62 63 ball 5; the exact numbers released. I used prior release numbers and the computer generator sheet from the office pool dated October 23, 2018. The reason I did not play the numbers was because I listened to a 9 year old, my son who said he did not believe they would play 28 again or that the last three numbers would be in consecutive order.

The closest my picks shown below are the 1 in the beginning and the 5 as the Mega Ball -- 1 5 15 18 22 ball 5. I did not play 61 at all but did play 62 and 63 on different lines.

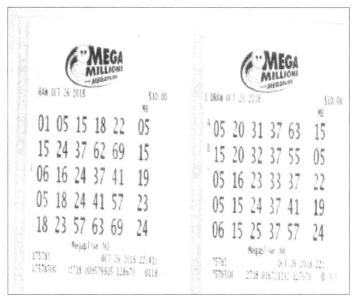

On this ticket dated October 23, 2018 I have noted 11-12 and 62 on line A. I believed the numbers for the October 26, 2019 draw would change to 61, 62 and 63. The first number would stay the same and ball would be 1 number higher than 4 a 5. Instead of 8 the previous 28 would be the second number. I was correct.

There were six other times that I predicted the numbers exactly in October and November of 2018. Those six times I did not play because two times I missed the closing of the Powerball draw by thinking I had until 10:45 pm to play, two other times I did play but misplaced my sheets with the numbers I intended to play after I feel asleep shortly before the drawing, and two other times I overslept.

One of the times I overslept after speaking with Virginia Lottery Commission fraud investigator Jerry Smith who claimed that the numbers were random, that I was a good guesser and that I would never get all of the numbers. The next drawing I had nearly the exact numbers based off mnemonics and a computer generated sheet I have dated October 24, 2018. I did not play that day because I was distracted by the statements of Jerry Smith and missed the closing of the lottery.

Several reasons I was never upset when I did not play numbers that were released was because I knew the lottery officials were tampering with the results and only allow exact numbers to be released when they choose. I told my children a month after the October 2018 winnings, with no new winnings, that the lottery officials would allow someone to win on Christmas and/or New Year's Eve.

This is done with a marketing scheme that is clear because it will cause new players to play for the first time and at least several drawings afterwards. Even if they never play again the increase in sales cover the amount paid to the winners.

Winners were announced on December 29, 2018 and January 1, 2019. So, prior to those two dates, I had the opportunity to likely win a large sum of money for picking some of the numbers but not the exact numbers because it was not on their timing for an exact winner.

The lottery officials only allow people to win on certain days that is why they close drawing at 15 minutes prior to the announcement of winning numbers. They do this to check who played what numbers and flip the winning numbers by either one or 10 to make the results not consisting of winning jackpot numbers.

Another way to ascertain when lottery officials are about to allow an exact winner is to look at random picks. When random picks are very similar they are not simply about to release numbers but are giving clues to their family, friends and associates that know of their scam.

My sons ages twelve and nine assisted me in discovering the patterns existing in winning numbers that allow you both predict lottery numbers and count the algorithms. The computer generated sheets counting 7 over by individual spaces and 17 over in blocks of 2 the numbers released on
January 1, 2019 is clear. 34 44 57 62 70 and the Powerball 14 is the first number on the line after 34 44 57.

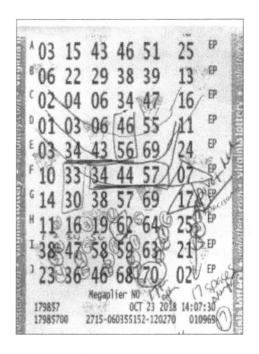

On October 30, 2018 and October 31, 2018 I played the numbers 34 44 57 61 repeatedly. I obviously believed that the numbers were due to be released. However, it was not time. My oldest son on October 26, 2018 picked 57 62 and 70 which are the last three numbers from the January 1st draw.

DRAW OCT 30 2018

11 20 30 45 61 08

Megaplier NO

1x3559   OCT 29 2018 10:29
15435900   2721-017270531-127470   019

$45 FALL CASH IS HERE AND OFFERS
A CHANCE TO WIN $5,000. ENTER $5 OR
MORE OF NON-WINNING PICK 3, PICK 4
AND CASH 5 TICKETS THRU OCT. VISIT
VALOTTERY.COM FOR DETAILS!
MEGA MILLIONS: OCT 30 $45 MILLION
POWERBALL: OCT 31 $40 MILLION

DRAW OCT 30 2018

11 20 30 45 61 08

Megaplier YES

83559   OCT 29 2018 10:30:
8355900   2721-053134714-125770   0101

$45 FALL CASH IS HERE AND OFFERS
A CHANCE TO WIN $5,000. ENTER $5 OR
MORE OF NON-WINNING PICK 3, PICK 4
AND CASH 5 TICKETS THRU OCT. VISIT
VALOTTERY.COM FOR DETAILS!
MEGA MILLIONS: OCT 30 $45 MILLION
POWERBALL: OCT 31 $40 MILLION

DRAW OCT 30 2018 $8.00

A **12 34 44 57 61 22**
B **12 34 44 57 61 22**
C **23 34 44 57 61 13**
D **23 34 44 57 61 03**

Megaplier NO

176425   OCT 30 2018 22:40:04
17642500   2722-050540314-123470   018788

DRAW OCT 30 2018

01 24 44 54 61 08
01 24 44 54 61 18

Megaplier NO

175785   OCT 30 2018 22:
17578500   2722-016813050-120570   0

$45 FALL CASH IS HERE AND OFFERS
A CHANCE TO WIN $5,000. ENTER $5 O
MORE OF NON-WINNING PICK 3, PICK 3

DRAW OCT 30 2018

MB

A 23 34 44 57 61   11
B 23 34 44 57 61   10

Megaplier YES

175785   OCT 30 2018 22
17578500   2722-019741467-120170

DRAW OCT 30 2018 $$.00

MB

A 23 34 44 57 61   08

Megaplier YES

175785   OCT 30 2018 22
17571500   2722-000009654-128170

DRAW OCT 30 2018

MB

A 23 34 45 57 61   18
B 23 34 45 57 61   08
C 23 34 45 57 61   03
D 23 34 45 57 61   01

Megaplier NO

176425   OCT 30 2018 22:41:16
17642500   2722-031685786-124070   019540

DRAW OCT 30 2018 $1.50

MB

A 23 34 44 57 61   18

Megaplier YES

175785   OCT 30 2018 22:30
17578500   2722-017764730-127770   019901

345 FALL CASH IS HERE AND OFFERS
A CHANCE TO WIN $5,000. ENTER $5 OR
MORE OF NON-WINNING PICK 3, PICK-4
AND CASH 5 TICKETS THRU OCT. VISIT
VALOTTERY.COM FOR DETAILS!
MEGA MILLIONS: OCT 30 $45 MILLION
POWERBALL: OCT 31 $40 MILLION

DRAW OCT 30 2018

23 34 44 57 61   2
23 34 44 57 61   2
23 34 44 57 61   0

Megaplier NO

176425   OCT 30 2018
17642500   2722-054714618-125970

345 FALL CASH IS HERE AND OFFE
A CHANCE TO WIN $5,000. ENTER
MORE OF NON-WINNING PICK 3, PIC
AND CASH 5 TICKETS THRU OCT. VI

DRAW OCT 30 2018

MB

A 12 34 44 57 61   11
B 12 34 44 57 61   10
D 12 34 44 57 61   0

Megaplier NO

75785   OCT 30 2018
17578500   2722-057742843-120770

345 FALL CASH IS HERE AND OFF
A CHANCE TO WIN $5,000. ENTER
MORE OF NON-WINNING PICK 3, P
AND CASH 5 TICKETS THRU OCT.
VALOTTERY.COM FOR DETAILS!
MEGA MILLIONS: OCT 30 $45 MIL
POWERBALL: OCT 31 $40 MILLION

DRAW OCT 30 2018 $1.00

MB

A 12 34 44 57 61   08

Megaplier YES

175785   OCT 30 2018 22:31
17578500   2722-053440283-125770

345 FALL CASH IS HERE AND OFFERS

DRAW OCT 30 2018 $8

MB

A 12 34 44 57 61   11
B 12 34 44 57 61   15
D 12 34 44 57 61   21
E 12 34 44 57 61   06

Megaplier NO

175785   OCT 30 2018 22:16:49
17578500   2722-057631259-127570   012040

DRAW OCT 30 2018 $3.00

MB

A 12 34 44 57 61   18

Megaplier YES

175785   OCT 30 2018 22:12:57
17578500   2722-037962010-120670   010240

DRAW OCT 30 2018 $2.00

MB

A 12 34 44 57 61   08

Megaplier NO

175785   OCT 30 2018 22:00:24
17578500   2722-004257306-125770   015045

345 FALL CASH IS HERE AND OFFERS
A CHANCE TO WIN $5,000. ENTER $5 OR
MORE OF NON-WINNING PICK 3, PICK 4
AND CASH 5 TICKETS THRU OCT. VISIT
VALOTTERY.COM FOR DETAILS!
MEGA MILLIONS: OCT 30 $45 MILLION
POWERBALL: OCT 31 $40 MILLION

MEGA MILLIONS

DRAW OCT 30 2018

MB

12 34 44 57 61   18

Megaplier NO

175785   OCT 30 2018 22:00
17578500

345 FALL CASH IS HERE AND OFFERS

It is clear that the lottery officials manipulate the numbers by ensuring that no one wins weekly. This is done by reviewing picks after the closing of the lottery.

It is also obvious that on October 30, 2018 and October 31, 2018 that my children and I picked numbers three months before they were released.

When I explained this to a man he asked, "How did you know they were going to be released on January 1, 2019?" The answer at that time was, "numerology" but now I can count the algorithms.

For each Powerball and Mega Millions draw that I played I used numerology as the first determination of what numbers to play. On January of 2019, I picked numbers based on numerology 3 and 34, and another two numbers in the 40s were followed. I fell asleep while working on numbers to pick and dreamt 34 57 62. I recognized those numbers from the computer generated sheet dated October 23, 2018, the numbers I played prior 34 44 57 on October 30th and 31st and combined them with the numbers my oldest son picked on the same day and picked 57 62 70.

On October 30, 2018 and October 31, 2018, I did not pick the exact numbers that were released but once I studied the past history of numbers released, the past numbers the children picked, the October 23, 2018 computer generated sheet, as well as random picks from the month of December 2018 I believed on January 1, 2019 34 44 57 62 70 was going to be released. On line A of my ticket I picked those correct numbers but the store employee deleted the numbers I picked and put an easy pick in the place.

I believed that consecutive numbers were going to be released for both the Mega Millions lotteries and the Pick 4. On line E of the ticket I have noted 34-57-62 which was three of the correct winning numbers. Line D also have consecutive numbers; 24-33-47-55-62 ball 3. When I contact 7-Eleven about this issue it was alleged that the store employee only worked that one day and never returned.

I also won $100.00 for the numbers I picked for pick 4 on the same night that predicted consecutive numbers for both draws. The night draw for the pick 4 was consecutive 2 3 4 5 which were not exact but out of order. I was able to stay home for two days so this gave me time to work on the numbers I picked.

I went to a 7-Eleven to get my tickets. At the 7-Eleven I saw the store employee reading my play slips and taking an extremely long time to insert my play slips into the machine. This was weird to me, I never seen someone do this before, so I immediately reviewed my tickets before I left. I immediately recognized that Line A were not the numbers I picked.

I attempted to put the numbers in place but was unable to do so because of exhaustion. Despite having the play slip with the correct numbers I predicted which the winning combinations I did not do what a normal person would do and simply look at the play slip and rewrite the numbers.

I initially thought that there was an error with the play slip and that I accidentally wrote the wrong numbers down. I did not have the sheets I used to predict the numbers because they were inadvertently left at home. The draw was about to close in a few minutes.

I then rationalized that maybe the error was part of the universe design so I played another ticket that matched a pattern similar to easy pick numbers on line A.

When I confronted the store employee about the numbers I picked being changed to an easy pick the employee stated that maybe something was wrong with the play slip so the computer automatically picked my numbers. Upon reviewing the numbers on the ticket I thought that the numbers erased were the numbers similar to numbers I obtained from two random people.

One of the numbers I obtained from two random people started with 8 then 18. However, I dropped the 8 on the other sheet and put 18 first with some of the same numbers I obtained but later voided those numbers. So, when I saw the random pick starting with 8 then 18 I believe that was the sheet with the numbers I voided and that caused the computer error.

However, that was false. It was after 10:45 that I reviewed my sheet and realized that I actually had all of the numbers on line A. When I asked the employee again how did it occur, and showed him the sheet he and another 7 Eleven employee said it was their error but maybe it would be good luck.

After the lottery released the numbers I picked but were sabotaged by the 7 Eleven employee and upon realizing the actions of some unknown individuals who caused my lottery picks to be replaced by an easy pick I prayed to the higher power. I prayed that the actions of these individuals be revealed and that even though I video recorded me picking the numbers that I get more proof that I knew the numbers, played the numbers and that the numbers were predictable.

I acquired these random picks that clearly reveal patterns and point to the numbers released on January 1, 2019. These tickets show that lottery officials use easy picks to communicate to the family, friends and associates winning numbers days prior to the draw.

The first number in the top left is 34 of the EP with 57 and 62 which are three numbers that I correctly predicted on line E. What is determinable is that I disregarded the other 2 numbers so I was able to discern which numbers were correct. Also is would not be surprising that 34 would be picked as the first number by myself.

In the bottom right corner, Line A is 23-30-51-58-70 ball 10 and Line B 16-18-42-44-49 is the random pick that co-workers had possession of. One of the co-workers was adamant in believing that I could not predict winning lottery numbers.

On Line E of my ticket played on January 1, 2019 line E is missing the 44 and 70 that is on the lottery ticket that was in possession of the co-workers. It is quite ironic that the co-workers easy pick have those missing numbers. If these individuals and others would have spent more time investigating the truth and working with me maybe the results would be different.

Instead of talking and rambling that I did not know what I was talking about I could have got assistance with playing at another location. Now, I realize after my son said that maybe the higher power did not want me to win at that time this is not true. I think many forces came against me to cause complications and the 7-Eleven employee changing my ticket was the last complication.

Part 3

The Use of Mnemonic to Predict Lottery Numbers

Auto|graph • Photo|graphic • Photo|graph

On 11/12/2018, I dreamed of numbers 360° with the degree symbol rotating extremely fast around the numbers 3, 6, 9 . I later discovered that my dreams and writings were using mnemonics to help me predict lottery numbers. The mind remembers "relatable" information. I then began to study how to master my memory to remember number patterns in the lotteries.

Photographs, Photographic, Autographs, Mnemonics all– gives as reminisced – topical or local memories

Graphs – original manuscripts – graph theory – a structure amounting to a set of objects" related" set of vertices and edifices – without error – diagram values

Autographs – auto-self - authors own manuscripts

Graphing – to write (to scratch)

Photograph – a drawing with a light
– lens focus visible wavelengths of light to a reproduction of what the human eye would see

Nicephone – niepce – camera obscure

Louis Daguerre – light sensitive iodine (invisible latent image)

Daguerreotype – with mercury fumes (light fast) bathed in hot salt solution removing the remaining silver iodide

Autograph -Authentic – indisputable without edits by
others
-authentic, verified by those familiar with
handwriting. (proof of origin)

Photographic Memory – recall text, numbers or similar in great detail (optima relate to life)
-the ability to remember information or visual images in great detail
-can take mental snapshots and recall the snapshots.
We piece together information and typically forget parts – remember gist, good.

Versus * counter this by remembering details at the time presented * Relate to what we already know

Eidetic Memory – recall with high precision (memories like a photograph/audio)

Episodic Memory – a type of long-term memory that refers to facts, data, or events that can be recalled at will

Hyperthymesia - a condition which leads people to be able to remember an abnormally large number of their life experiences in vivid detail

Mnemonics –Art of Memory – principle of order – memory device, any learning technique that aid information retention or retrieval (remembering) in the human memory. –use to encode information – associate it with something more accessible or meaningful

Mnemosyne – remembrance – natural v. artificial = inborn v. trained and developed

-use constants by figures = numbers by words to creative associates remembered

At the beginning of predicting lottery numbers I could only figure out numbers by the use of mnemonics. I used information relevant to my life which included my birthday, my children's birthday and religious dates and information. One example is the prediction I made of the November 10, 2018 draw of 05-29-34-53-57 ball 24

I listed the following information:

1.) Power ball will be 5 or 4 /9?345
2.) 2. And 3 gives 5/5/5
3.) For turn back on (5)
4.) 4/5 or 4/4)
5.) 4 double down by 5 (4)/(5)
6.) 3 confront 4 34/22 (double cross)
7.) Tell 4 to turn back to (4/5)
8.) 45° 5/0th
9.) 6/3not in coordinates
10.) 9 power of 5
11.) 37
12.) 3x3x3
13.) 4 professed 3 times
14.) 56 minutes, 4 to tell = 60 minutes
15.) 10 power the 2things
16.) 2121/02
17.) 16 29-31/24/ 3100
18.) 1657 "4603" 25.770 complete rotation
19.) 5
20.) 4 (2/2) 3ı 6

Part 4
Master Language/ Speech /Computer Science

Master Sound - Thus the Universe -

Computer Programing – computing, developing hardware/software – to process/manage information

Synonymous- counting and calculating

Communication – act of conveying meaning through mutual symbols and rules

-Making sense of the presumed original message

1.) motive, reason
2.) message
3.) encoding
4.) transmission by assigned medium
5.) noise sources – send to others to receive
6.) reception reassembling from the sequence of received signals
7.) Interpretation and making sense

Philology – oral and written history

Semiotics – study of signs and it processes

LINGUISTIC –scientific study of language
–analyze language

Form – what is it, how it works

Meaning –signifiers words, phrases, signs and symbols, what is the denotation

Context – circumstances that form the setting for an event, states or idea, to fully understand communication

Determine how does it relate to our processes

Grapheme- the smallest unit of a writing system

Phonology – system of sounds - a homophone – unit of sound that distinguishes one word from another (Allophones)

Morphology – forms of words

Syntax- the set of rules, principles and processes that govern the structure sentences, compounds, homo-syno, anto-hypermetric, mero, holo(nymy)

Semantics – the study of the meaning of words, phrases, longer forms of expression –paragraphed structure and punctuation

Phonograph Phonetic – representation of each speech sound with a single symbol (as close to how they actually sound)

LEXICOLOGY

Phonetic – <u>Synchronic</u> – History <u>Diachronic</u> – change in time

HOW – <u>Onomasiology</u> – take an idea and ask for its names (what is the name)

WHAT – <u>Semasiology</u> – start with a word and ask what it means (what is the meaning)

WHEN – <u>Etymology</u> – history/origin (how change over time)

WHERE – <u>Morphology</u> – form of words

WHY – <u>Pragmatic</u> – system of why – how context contributes to meaning

SYNTAX OF LANGUAGE – Lexicology – form, meaning , use of words

<u>Syntax</u> – arrangements of words and phrases to create well formed sentences

<u>Pragmatic</u> -context contributes to meaning

<u>Etymology</u> – history/origin of words (change), rules, ordered operation, depend on context

SYNTAX OF MATH - symbols and strings of Symbols – well formed formulas v. formal systems

COMPUTER PROGRAMING

Computer programing – rules governing the composition of well-formed expressions in a programming language.

Expression – a finite combination of symbols that is well formed according to rules that depend on the context (multiplication is higher than addition)

> ACM Circula 2005 – goal oriented structured activity structured -make behave intelligently

> 1989 ACM report computing as discipline -study algorithms

Computer Science – Syntax – rules governing the composition of well-formed expression in a programming language

Parenthesis language – synthetic consultant – condition – then expression //@

Mathematical Logic – Language = Programming Language – formal, set of instructions, produce an output

Basic master "Hello, World!" program First – it is created, programs that implement algorithms

Limited set of specific instructions v. rather than general programming languages

First – programs directed behavior (could not produce different behavior in response to input or condition)

<u>Now</u> – **Imperative** – a sequence of operations to perform

Declarative – a desired result is specified, not how to achieve it

C programming ISO Standard – language specified other than per – have dominant implementation; treatise as a reference.

Some both –standards and extensions taken from the dominant implementation being common

Implementation – perform written action in that language

Compilation – a compiler takes as input a program in some language, and translate (may be multiple passes) like Code Generation

Code Generation aka algorithms

-process, compiler's code generation converts some intermediate representation of source code into a form (e.g machine code) that is executed by computer.

Algorithms – organization by an architect to change by targets identified/program

Parse Tree – reflex the syntax of imprinted language

Abstract Syntax Tree – source code written in a programming language

Part 5

Traveling Paths
To Predict Lottery Numbers

The Path of Redemption

1,2,3 – as easy as 1, 2, 3

The Road less traveled, but wrong path

These number paths are actual algorithm paths for counting Powerball and Mega Millions winning lottery numbers. I used these paths of numbers earlier on to predict winning number; it is mnemonics I used to predict the winning lottery numbers.

1.) **Pattern 1**–1,2,3 then 9 is the easiest route to God. But this is path rare.
2.) **Pattern 2** – 1, 2, 4, 8, 7, 5
3.) **Pattern 3** – Points 1, 2, 3, 7, 8, to 9
4.) **Pattern 4** – 3, 6 (when 3 and 6 are together 9 controls – based on duality in 3rds) and 9 is omnipotent and the goal once reached start the number anew.

Numerous others paths based on taking the wrong turns or standing too long at one point results in myriad paths. Patterns 1 to 4 are basic paths.

If rough times occur you will have to go back two steps If you stay on 6 to long or travel back to many times will have to go back to one.

If you go back to six three times it is nearly impossible to bounce back. You will have to go back to one – the very beginning.

The normal, average life travel is a learning process where you travel on the circle of life reaching different points to reach enlighten which is the last point at point 9. You may get to 9 to soon but will have to restart at a point that is determined by where you got off track at..
Points 1, 2, 3, 7, 8, to 9

1, 2, 4 to 9 is the faster route traveled by a few – a short cut that will likely cause problems because step 3 is important.

One step forward, two steps back.

Best path to enlightenment: Points 1, 2, 3 to 9

2nd best path to enlightenment: Points 1 , 2, 3 to 8, 9

3rd best path to enlightenment: Points 1, 2, 3, 4, 9

Unnatural: Points 1, 2,3, 4

STATE OF CONFUSION/ TURNING POINT
ARE AT POINT 4 AND 5 :
Points 1, 2, 3, 4, 5/0

4, 5/0, 8 is the best choice but usually does not occur because it a step to far if not ready

4, 5/0, 7 going one step backwards 8 should have been next but may have to travel pass 7 to get prepared

4, 5/0, 6 going in the wrong direction, to hell

If you get to 0 you should go straight to 8 but from 5 7 is fine. But go back 1. Back to 1 5 to 7 back to 1 or 8

1 and 8 gets to 9 (1) is longer route.

Go to 1, 2, 3 skip 4

Go to 5 create confusion and could lead to 0/nothing or 6 evil.

1,2,3, to 7 or 9

1,2,3 0, then 7 or 9

1, 2, 3, to 9 – Best route - but rare and road less traveled

1,2,3, to 7 get rest 8 (because skip 5, 6) then day of new beginning 9 (enlightenment)

Part 6

The Meaning of Numbers

The truth of numbers surrounds us daily:

Number 1

1. The beginning of it all **1**
2. Restart over at point **1**
3. Back to square **1**
4. **1** track mind
5. **1** good turn deserves another
6. If it is not **1** thing it is another
7. Take care of number **1**
8. Do **1** better
9. All-in-**1**

Number 2

1. It takes **2**
2. **1** plus 1 will always equal **2**
3. **2** peas in a pod
4. one cannot be in **2** places at once
5. be as **2** minds about everything
6. Tell me one or **2**
7. it takes **2** to tango
8. Next stop to faith 1 + 1 = **2**
9. It takes **2** to get to 3

Number 3

1. and baby makes **3**
2. Children, one is one, two is fun and **3** is a full house
3. Good things comes in **3**s
4. **3**rd time lucky
5. **3**'s a charm
6. we **3** shall meet again
7. **3** wise men
8. give **3** cheers
9. **3** basic skills

Number 4

1. Cast to the **4** winds
2. **4** corners of the earth
3. **4** leaf clover
4. If stuck put 2 and 2 together to get **4**
5. on all **4**s
6. to be **4** cats
7. **4** square behind

Number 5

1. to be in the **5**th pine
2. **5** finger discount
3. take **5**
4. **5** will get you ten
5. **5** o'clock shadow
6. full fathom **5** the father lies
7. Platinum sombreros
8. take **5**

Number 6

1. confused at **6** and sevens
2. **6** feet under
3. **6** of one, half a dozen of the other
4. deep **6**
5. watch your **6**
6. hit for **6**
7. knocked for **6**
8. **6** and two threes
9. **6** degrees of separation

Number 7

1. **7** day wonder
2. lucky number **7**
3. the magnificent **7**
4. One year's seeds make **7** years weeds
5. **7** league boots
6. **7** year itch
7. **7**th heaven

Number 8

1. **8** ways to Sunday
2. two four six **8** who do we appreciate
3. behind the **8** ball
4. pieces of **8**
5. to be cooler than an **8**

Number 9

1. on cloud **9**
2. **9** times out of ten
3. **9** days wonder
4. dressed to the **9**s
5. **9** times out of ten
6. a stich in time saves **9**
7. whole **9** yards

Letter value – physics to words

a |1|2|b|=

1 pattern – 1, 2, 4, 8, 7, 52 pattern – 3 & 6 = magnet field

3 & 6 together 9 controls (based on duality in 3rds) and 9 is omnipotent

3 & 6 and 1, 2, 4, 8, 7, 5 [3rd] (based on ten number system)

3 & 6 – separating dimensions, 4th higher power (vortex at line of 5/0) [13:13]

3, 9, 6 693 9339

3	6

Each side, represent 9 curves to get to enlightenment and the trinity different dimensions

3, 6, 12, 1+2=3, 12x2=24, 2+6=8, 22 to power 2= 248, 4+8=12, 1+2=3

64 cycle, 64= 128

1+2+8=11 (clockwise)

1+1=2

FLOW OF ENERGY

1, 2, ,4, 9~

~ 7, 5, 1 $\rightarrow$

Doubling circuits of b^2. 3x3x3

9 5/0 circular motion

9/6/3 spiral motion

3,6,
9

1+1=2, 2+2=4, $4b^2=8$ (=) 16 (also equivalent to 6+1= 7 pattern)

pt.1 (**1**) to pt.2 (**2**), to pt. 3 (**3**) to pt.4 (**8**)

$16^2=32$ pt.1 to pt.2 (7), to pt. 3 (5) to pt.4 (1)

3+2=5   (7)   (5)   (1)   (0) reaching for 9

$3^2 = 64$

6+4=10

1+0 = 1

Numbers boxed together

1	2	3
4	5	6
7	8	9

3, 6, 9 do not connect – 9 controls = oscillation ▲ trinity with a curve

Evaluate

1.)   positive energy flows
2.)   negative energy flows
3.)   letters of order
4.)   opposite versus attractions and
5.)   degrees of angles

KEYS TO MASTER THE UNIVERSE
9 = 9

LISTEN I AM HERE!
PERFECT – NUMBER 9 – NONE EQUALS

UNITY OF BOTH SIDES (GOOD WITH THE BAD)
– linear – Never changing

On top, solo, no trinity but higher – all of the power, in control 3, 6, 9 work in collaboration
-understand this, you will master the universe.

A fingerprint is the look of a blue print of God.
9 is the universe itself, it is energy, vibration

9=9
↑~↑ always return here

All multiples are the same
9x1 =9
9x2=18
   equivalent to
         then 9x3=27
            2+7=9
1+8=9

1 + 8
2 + 7
4 + 5

9

Φ

9 is at the center – controller of it all, energy, life
– draws you to seek its source
Physics = Physical = Energy
Numbers, people, higher power #9 with 3 and 6

9 with 3 and 6 is creation of balance symmetrical illusion
– distort reality

Without (9) everything would not exist
Everything wraps around, coil – energy drawn to
Only if you open your heart and minds and seek me

9x1=9	0+9=9
9x2=18	1+8=9
9x3=27	2+7=9
9x4=36	3+6=9
9x5=45	4+5=9
9x6=54	5+4=9
9x7=63	6+3=9
9x8=72	7+2=9
9x9=81	8+1=9

THE MEANING OF 9

PERFECT NUMERICAL ORDER
PUSH TOWARD ENLIGHTMENT

Question: Why is 5 after 4 – A reason exists for all numbers

4 x 4 means? = 5 due to symmetry

Good v. Evil

The higher power did not create but obviously left space for evil.

A choice. Free will. Numbers explain it all.

Without free will you will be a machine
Without emotion, you are a machine.

Creativity comes from senses. Cannot have sense without bad experiences existing.

You as a machine without senses cannot be human. You must feel pain. Do not have to experience but would never have happiness, fulfillment if you do not understand the opposite.

1x4=4
2x4=8
3x4=12
4x4=16
5x4=20
6x4=24

9 x 1 =	9
9 x 2 =	18
9 x 3 =	27
9 x 4 =	36

9 X 5 = 45

1+2=3
1+6=7
2+0=2
2+4=6

7x4=28 but 2+8=10 and 1+0=1

8x4=32

9x4=36

9 X 10 = 90

↑ ~ ↑

3+6=9   Master this and you will obtain enlightenment

The meaning of 1

$$1 \times 5 = 5$$

1 x 1 =	1	1 x 6 =	6
1 x 2 =	2	1 x 7 =	7
1 x 3 =	3	1 x 8 =	8
1 x 4 =	4	1 x 9 =	9

$$1 \times 10 = 10$$

The meaning of 2

2 X 5 =10			
2 x 1 =	2	2 x 6 =	12
2 x 2 =	4	2 x 7 =	14
2 x 3 =	6	2 x 8 =	16
2 x 4 =	8	2 x 9 =	18

2 X 10 = 20

The meaning of 3

1, 2, 4

3 X 5 = 15

3 x 1 =	3	3 x 6 =	18
3 x 2 =	6	3 x 7 =	21
3 x 3 =	9	3 x 8 =	24
3 x 4 =	12	3 x 9 =	27

3 X 10 = 30

1+2=3
2+4=6
4+8=12
8+7=15
7+5=12
5+1=6
1+2=3

1+2=3
1+5=6
1+2=3

The meaning of 4

Good vs. Evil (4/5)

Duality = Good/Evil * Right/Wrong * Love/Hate

	4 X 5 = 20		
4 x 1 =	4	4 x 6 =	24
4 x 2 =	8	4 x 7 =	28
4 x 3 =	12	4 x 8 =	32
4 x 4 =	16	4 x 9 =	36
	4 X 10 = 40		

4	20 is the power of 4	24
8	Center of 4	28
12	Unity of 4	32
16	Half to	36

4, 8, 3, 7, 2, 2, 6, 1, 5

Opposite attracts. Ends in 5 (4 to 5)

4 attraction to 9 by the center, power of 20

6+1= 7

1 + 5 = 5 5+1=6   20 is the power generator of 4 to enlightenment. 1+5/5 is a conductor. Center outward similarities

10/20

167, 297, 4

Evil was not created to harm but to understand what you have, can do and push towards the light

3	
7	
2	Master key to understand law of attraction
6	
10	GOOD v EVIL
1	
5	
9	

Duality transitions – number of duality 4 and 5 or 5/0

```
        1    2    3

     You │God and │Your Partner
```

Step 1 Take a leap of faith

Step 2 – duality need to join with partner – 2 minds work better than one. God is there for you (3)

Everyone has a holy trinity of 3. 3 =your soul mate (have to at step)

3 is always the answer, step 1, step 2, step 3 - If all else fails try, a 2nd time than a third time

45° duality, angle that we fight- put on that breast plate get ready for the awaken. 6+3 = the council of good. The council lost by 3 because Satan. So God triple a counter – attack by half 3x3x3 to defeat Satan.

After speaking with 5 for confirmation it will be revealed that 4 doubled crossed – A sell out – do not give in, Satan is a trickster.

The meaning of 5

THE REASON OF EVIL

BALANCE, FULLFILLMENT

Why evil attracts = good vs. evil

-The Numbers explain it all -

$$5 \times 5 = 25$$

5 x 1 =	5	5 x 6 =	30
5 x 2 =	10	5 x 7 =	35
5 x 3 =	15	5 x 8 =	40
5 x 4 =	20	5 x 9 =	45

$$5 \times 1 = 50$$

You will know WHAT LOVE IS

-without would not understand hate

-without would not understand loss

-without would not understand emptiness

Dark matter is in the center – 1.) creation simply a burst of energy 2.) you are the universe

Out of nothing, darkness a power like no other created YOU with love

But due to lack of communication with human beings the force has been separated from the force. It is simply all in the numbers.

9 1,2,3,4,5,6,7,8   9   1,2,3,4,5,6,7,8,   9

9 2,4,6,8,1,3,5,7   5/0   2,4,6,8,1,3,5,7   9

9 4,8,3,7,2,6,1,5   4,8,3,7,2,6,1,5,   9

891

7502

54

9

←center out→

5/0 stop turn around, now. When you get to 5 understand you are at a low point.

5/0 similar to yin and yang – A thin line between love and hate. 5/4 opposites but 5 is the ultimate low point that if 4 is energy of love. 5 is energy to nothing.

165   297   438

9 is on an AXIS – 9 is a perfect point of existence

$8\sim1$

$7\sim2$

$5\sim4$

Back and forth

Balance must exist. This is the reason evil exist because without you cannot exist. (will sustain, experience joy

Happiness/Sad

Up/Down

Left/Right

Yes/No

The meaning of 6

	6 X 5 = 30			
	6 x 1 =	6	6 x 6 =	36
3,6, 36, 63	6 x 2 =	12	6 x 7 =	42
3+6=9	6 x 3 =	18	6 x 8 =	48
6+3+9	6 x 4 =	24	6 x 9 =	54
	6 X 10 = 60			

1+2+3+4+5+6+7+8+9=45 are numbers 1 to 9 added together separately. It is the same as 4+5 =9 = circle of life

Includes and excludes = same time/simultaneously = 3, 6

The meaning of 7

7 X 5 = 35

7 x 1 =	7	7 x 6 =	42
7 x 2 =	14	7 x 7 =	49
7 x 3 =	21	7 x 8 =	56
7 x 4 =	28	7 x 9 =	63

7 X 10 = 70

The meaning of 8

$$8 \times 5 = 40$$

8 x 1 =	8	8 x 6 =	48
8 x 2 =	16	8 x 7 =	56
8 x 3 =	24	8 x 8 =	64
8 x 4 =	32	8 x 9 =	72

$$8 \times 10 = 80$$

Part 7
How It All Adds Together

The meaning of 3, 6, 9
with 0/5 & 9

Look at things from all angles.

But you still end back at 9.

Enlightenment – It all started from darkness; a sudden
burst of light, air, gases, = DNA formula.
– came from darkness and light – it is
within us; but light is supposed to
outshine darkness.

360

-are supposed to be able to Evaluate,
-Look at things from all angles
-Determine right from wrong
-Ascertain the truth from the false – EASILY

180

The sum of all digits excluding 9 = 36   9 is/= 36 or 0

360° = Universe

with perfect symmetry

1+2+3+4+5+6+7+8=36   (3+6=9)

9 plus any digit = the same as the digit added to nine

9+5= 14   (1+4=5)

9+8= 17   (1+7=8)

9+7= 16   (1+6=7)

Angles, Degrees, Stars = **360° the universe** – earth is just one part of the universe

360° is a circle
3+6+0+0=9

180°
1+8+0=9

90°
9+0=9

45°
4+5=9
(4 lines in between 8 total line)

22.5
2+2+5=9
(3(4) times 12 lines in between 16=4x4)

11.25° (1+1+2+5=9)

5.625° (5+6+2+5=18) (1+8=9)

2.8125° (2+8+1+2+5=18) (1+8=9)

POLYGONS

Sun Rays, Angles, Vibrations
(Angles to reach Enlightenment)

Opposite / vectors – 9 is the center of it all

60°

x3

180°   (1+8=9)

90°

x4

360° (3+6=9)

180°

x5

900° (5+4+0 =9)

120°

<u>x6</u>

720° (7+2+0=9)

135°

<u>x 8</u>

1080° (1+0+8+0=9)

140°

<u>x 9</u>

1260°(1+2+6+0=9)

144°

<u>x 10</u>

1440° (1+4+4+0=9)

Star of David and 360

6 sides

6 angles

equilateral triangle is 60°

6, 6, 6

Count the # of the beast - # of a man 6 score and 6

2 triangles 1 is right side up and upside down (breast and sexual organs)

Mid-section = appetite when enlightened- head filled with spiritual enlightenment

Head – reflects spiritual wisdom

Love-peace, happiness, joy

Concord, agreement

Of the carnal minds – envy, jealousy, enmity, hatred, strife, murder, war

The MEANING OF LIFE/UNIVERSE

Answer to Creation – Answer to is there a God Answer found in Numerology

There are 63 orders of magnitude = Powers of 10 =40

Plimpton 3, 22 (tablet)

3x3x3=

   27   27/42

7, 9

8, 12, 22, 23, 24 9

10, 27,42,10, 42

Two physical contacts

Base 13   13/42

               ↓

         4, 13 + 2

7, 16, 19

3, 4, 11, 24, 42

5, 12, 25, 36, 42 (10)

SECOND SPHENIC

20, 30

Goldberg conjecture = 6, 13, 36

Binary logarithm

1, 2, 5 base 2m

Power 2 is 10

3231 (65-11) 11 80,000 -2

Hitches guide to the Galaxy = 1 ,2 ,4, 18, 66

Part 8

Harmony In Numbers

HOW NUMBERS WILL BE USED TO CRUSH SATAN

Working in 5 by 5 for the purpose to defeat Satan

Satan, while at 3 by 3 will be crushed by the power of 9 at a 45° angle

4 1) Is only a human heart 2) still my child with 3 – take your power and combine with 30 (1, 2, 3, then 5, 10, 15)

4 is tricked by 0 a nothing

3 times you pay 1 by 1 by 1 (by 3) over 4 tell him 1) love 2) father, and 3) son. Let him make a choice. 1) Do it with love 2.) no animosity

Then 3 go to 5 to confer 1.) plan 2.) discuss with 4, let 4 make a choice

9 phase (each) rotation power of god is magnified

By 1 person

Things at that time is done by (5ths) –(this is not human fifths)

But on accord with 5 others. [5 = 0, 5 against Satan] Satan who is nothing but a fool.]

But you need 5 for harmony, to stay centered. To crush Satan like no other. While making plans to turn against the higher force Satan was warned **3** times to not go forward with his plans. He went and got 3. Then 3 got 3. Satan was warned again 3 times but still he turned against the higher force and by 3 +2 the explosion occurred

Core doubled if a power like no other 5 = by 5s

5
10
15
20
25
30
35
40

45

45° angle is when you get to the 4th person on your warrior team. The sun will rise in the North at 3:33 am. A time of awaken.

Let all that want to hear. All that want to see search and find your light. You have 3 more choices with 5 the 5th

POWER OF NUMBERS

		1 X 5 = 5	
1 x 1 =	1	1 x 6 =	6
1 x 2 =	2	1 x 7 =	7
1 x 3 =	3	1 x 8 =	8
1 x 4 =	4	1 x 9 =	9
		1 X 10 = 10	

		2 X 5 = 10	
2 x 1 =	2	2 x 6 =	12
2 x 2 =	4	2 x 7 =	14
2 x 3 =	6	2 x 8 =	16
2 x 4 =	8	2 x 9 =	18
		2 X 10 = 20	

		3 X 5 = 15	
3 x 1 =	3	3 x 6 =	18
3 x 2 =	6	3 x 7 =	21
3 x 3 =	9	3 x 8 =	24
3 x 4 =	12	3 x 9 =	27
		3 X 10 = 30	

4 X 5 = 20			
4 x 1 =	4	4 x 6 =	24
4 x 2 =	8	4 x 7 =	28
4 x 3 =	12	4 x 8 =	32
4 x 4 =	16	4 x 9 =	36
4 X 10 = 40			

5 X 5 = 25			
5 x 1 =	5	5 x 6 =	30
5 x 2 =	10	5 x 7 =	35
5 x 3 =	15	5 x 8 =	40
5 x 4 =	20	5 x 9 =	45
5 X 10 = 50			

6 X 5 = 30			
6 x 1 =	6	6 x 6 =	36
6 x 2 =	12	6 x 7 =	42
6 x 3 =	18	6 x 8 =	48
6 x 4 =	24	6 x 9 =	54
6 X 10 = 60			

	7 X 5 = 35		
7 x 1 =	7	7 x 6 =	42
7 x 2 =	14	7 x 7 =	49
7 x 3 =	21	7 x 8 =	56
7 x 4 =	28	7 x 9 =	63
	7 X 10 = 70		

	8 X 5 = 40		
8 x 1 =	8	8 x 6 =	48
8 x 2 =	16	8 x 7 =	56
8 x 3 =	24	8 x 8 =	64
8 x 4 =	32	8 x 9 =	72
	8 X 10 = 80		

	9 X 5 = 45		
9 x 1 =	9	9 x 6 =	54
9 x 2 =	18	9 x7 =	63
9 x 3 =	27	9 x 8 =	72
9 x 4 =	36	9 x 9 =	81
	9 X 10 = 90		

THE ULTIMATE GOAL – CONNECT THE DOTS

(aka STARS) ALIGNMENTS
ASTROLOGY

CHOAS = DEVIL = EPLURIUS

There is even order out of chaos.

An Awakening: <u>Euphoric.</u> It is never smooth. The knowledge is overwhelming. (soul to soul)

<u>33°</u> spine – energy – brain

4th Dimension Awaken

Body – mind – soul   Higher Elevation (7 spiral/gate -Hermitic) <u>alleviation</u> zig zag to crown Davinair

UNDERSTANDING DEITIES TO DE-CODE LOTTERY

Epic of Gilgamesh (c. 1200 BC)

Blood type – Anunnaki - underworld

Utnapishting immortal / survivor of the Great Flood, (A) set world on flames

<u>NABU</u>- the God of literacy – Nebo in bible Isaiah 46:1/Jeremiah 48:1
    -syncretized with Apollo
    -linked Mercury/Thorth (wisdom)

Old Babylonia Period (18:30-BC – 1531)

A new set of deities known as Igigi introduced/

The Poem of Erra – distinction

Between the two; Akkadian and Atraḥasis

6 generations of Gods forced to perform labor for – Igigi – heaven, deities the Annunnaki: After 40 days, rebel.

God ends creates humans to replace them.

An- the Sumerian – God of the Sky

a-nuna, a-nuna-ke, or a-nun-na, "primarily off spring" or "offspring of An" (offspring of An & Ki-each Goddesses)

Enlil – God of Air – at his birth heaven and earth were in separable.

Heaven and earth were (cleaved) in two and carried away the earth Enil.

Carried away the sky An (father of Enil)

Nabi-spokesman – Aaron for Moses Exodus 7:1 – different places, locations

"Assembly of Gods" through which the Gods made all of the decisions. Counterpart to the semi-democratic legislative system that existed during the Third Dynasty of UR (c. 2112 BC – c. 2004 B.C.)

(7)

1.) An – equatorial, sky

2.) Enlil – Northern sky

Enki- Southern sky

Ninhursag

Nanna – moon

Utu – sun

Inanna – planet Venus

Ishtar – the east Semitic equivalent to Inanna

Poem Enki and the World Order

Enlil- Northern Sky – path of Enlil's celestial orbit was a continuous, symmetrical circle around the north celestial pole

But those of An and Enki were believed to intersect at various points.

Akkadian, Babylonia and Assyrian – a reverence begets favors, sacrifice prolongs life and prayer atones guilt. He who fears the Gods is not slighted. He who fears the Arnummaki extends his days – Babylonia Hymn

Record Keeping Calendar

"Seven Luminaries" – 4 seasons

1 0, Φ °|°, b², 1+1=2, 3x3x3, 360°, 369,

<u>7 days, 7 planets</u>

1.)   Monday – Moon
2.)   Tuesday-Mars
3.)   Wednesday-Mercury
4.)   Thursday-Jupiter
5.)   Friday- Venus
6.)   Saturday – Saturn
7.)   Sunday –Sun

Byzantine Calendar 7626-7527
Month – Motion of Moon

29.53 cycles of moon phases (lunation)
Are synodic months

<u>Maya, Zep, Tepi, Kali, Lugo</u>

<u>Eco System</u>: Gold, Silver

Bronze and Iron Age
Telescope = Satan
2150 yr. New Zodiac
26, 500 completion

Cygus – diety 70 11, 500 AD

Near Lyra (Vega) 13, 700 AD

At the 45° angle (look to the North Star) – 5 by 5 by 5 = 5 points by 5 times

Stars will look faint until 4, gets his angle together with the 5 points and has 24 hours (1) day

00 doubled against Satan

Draco the Dragon – change 29'09 from (0.45/25) 45 power of 9 of the 5

27, 3x3x3, rotation 360°

Heros Gams – <u>Get Awoke</u> – an awakening. **<u>Balance</u>** both sides, left and right of the brain -will find in them without.

Blockages closed – takes years/ lifetimes (WAKE UP)
Knowledge and Truth = Power

You have to seek knowledge of all:

1.)   Religions
2.)   Quantum physics
3.)   Astronomy
4.)   Astrology
5.)   Occult
6.)   Herbs
7.)   Electromagnetic fields

"Magnum Opus" – inner knowing of -magnetic push & pull [lay lines]

Negative & positive forces (EKG machine – heart produced energy)

-will be drawn to
-lifetime after lifetime until we get it right
Dogmas |
Tech Age | Nature
Toxic – Halide – Pineal bland (neuro transmitters

DMT all to cause you to have a low IQ to make docile.

OUR RELATIONSHIP TO THE PLANETS

ENERGY WAVES and the PERFECTLY DESIGNED WORDS

Electricity – our connection to water -All planets, create frequencies – alignments of cycles

Words are powerful, pitch <u>SWORD</u> – cast words, letters are sacred ideas

Word Play – Find the Hidden Meaning

Tricks – Manipulate words & meaning of words same

Occult

Death

<u>Contract</u>- Trick - so is a Treatise – Agreement to do a fraudulent document

[Cross of Saint George – Inquisition – goal keep masses illiterate)]

Pine cones & Serpent

1. First Souls
2. Human Spirits
v. Government, fraud by concealing information operating without full disclosure

Chi & Pinea

> Pineal Gland
> -production of neurotransmitters
> -facilitate altered states of awakening
> -spiritual enlightenment

Magi – Magnetic – manipulate forces

Sound - create structures, building blocks

Golden Halo – **<u>Golden Age</u>** – higher thought – Spiritual Perception

Woman on lunar cycle – Aggression full moon – water as a conduct – electrical field – salt water

Copper v Iron Gods hold rods

Part 9

If All Else Fails Try, Try Again

1st try – 2nd try – 3rd try

You Are Either With Or Against Me 3=25
Let Me Know Today

11 = God, God's council and you - (God + council of 9 = 10)

North Star –guides and angles

The universe is the center the Core 360°

36° 0 sum of all numbers excluding the 3x3x3 3 is =25

$9b^2$ $9b^2$ = duality = 9+9=18 - Male and female 3 holy trinity)
(50 years of transition)

3	18	3|6	45	50	(5)

6	To the right
3	To the left

9 x 9 = 81
1   6
2   7
3   5   8
4   9
Grid of Faith

= 9 (they are putting it backwards - know that it is really *63*

At <u>4's</u> weakest moment 4 was tricked by a nobody, Satan, a lying conniving snake.

1, 2, 3, take your power. 4 combined with 5. The universe will set in perfect alliance. 4 has a need in his heart. Find out his angle use it for his best interest and the greater good.

4 is a master. Every one of the devil hates a master.

A master will get 5 (this will add up to perfection 9 – All for his greater good)

3x3x3 = 27

6+1=7   6 plus the greatest 1

He needs humans to pair with angles for duality = b^2

He made a mistake believing that a robot will make him the greatest but those who love <u>4</u>

Where Did God Come From?

I am friction rubbed together by sound, rotation and angles.

Master Plan: How do friction work?

If there was something to create God than the person referred to or believed to be God cannot be the higher power. He would be a master of many masters.

So with you he spoke; cannot be the higher power because speaking is a creation that exists for a purpose. The purpose is to communicate with others.

The higher force is not a person, a place or thing. It is something but nothing however everything that creation derived from.

If he came from nothing, how could that be? Now you have been told a LIE.

You can get something for nothing, something from nothing and 1 + 1 will always be 2;
But I will not ever need anything to be me.

I am a force, a straight line, not nothing but a frequency; a pitch.

Like a horizon at a beach, look at that guess what -- I am me.

(Remember when you sat at the beach and prayed and I sent you the meditating elephant your way?)

Did you throw it back?
In the water is life. In that water is me.
I am friction rubbed together, as you created me.
From a tree, from this earth,
Beyond the horizon was I. **UNCOUNTED TIME**.

Alpha and Omega = beginning and end, the end is the beginning and the beginning will never be an end.

Because it is a rotation, vibration, energy and sound. Listen very closely, follow your heart, watch your dreams, and the time you awake. Be humble. Be kind. Be free to explore your mind. (3:05), (3,6,9), (3669)

For your thoughts are I and I are you. No accident don't get me wrong because wrong can be right, be point on time. But I am not time, not place or matter -- I master these.

A FORCE LIKE NO OTHER

For dual purposes

True north – a line terminating in a five pointed star.

Divided (division sign) (0) all visible (angels) directed into two those that intersect and those that do not. (known & unknown)

Never meant to comprehend while on earth because we are to master this life first. (Can't even get that right but you have to move to the next step.)

Take one step at a time because while on earth it will never happen. How the force simply exist is not for us to know now. Like the horizon, human beings have limits of range or perception, knowledge, of the universe and what is beyond it.

Where you stand on earth has no viewpoint to know what the higher force is.

WHAT IS THE HIGHER FORCE

A force that existed before it all (in alter, two events)
– created by a master of masters

The moving object (that was formerly at rest), moved across another object (the object were opposite of each other) 0+1=1 1+1 = 2

A force – that holds back the movement as a sliding object, resist the relative motion or tendency to such motion of two bodies or substances in contact

Friction – the resistance that one surface or object encounters when moving over another "a lubricating system that reduces friction" – the action of one surface or object rubbing against another - conflict or animosity caused a clash of will, temperaments or opinions.

The force was not created it is 1.) External, 2.) Omnipresent, 3) Immaterial, 4.) Invisible

Can't be touched, seen or smelled – never changes, only external now, has always been, never randomly occurred, is everywhere; not material

Time = a measure of change
Matter = finite, was created had to begin
Space = only a certain amount of distance

Constant rotation= co-efficient of friction mu ( )

Measured in units of force co-efficient = f/l

Of friction is dimensionless (MLT-2) = kgm/s² like a horon (a division sign) invisible not for your perception, 360° azimuth, angles of possible directions. Of true North.

1.) Embodies evil light and friction generates (FGmax flat surface n=mg normal force) or evolves heat 2.) live light; rest dark

If one doubles the load being moved, friction increases by 2. <u>Friction</u> is directly proportional to the weight of the load being moved.

A New Horizon – Is Me - A New Day

IT IS A THIN LINE – INTERSCETION OF DAY AND NIGHT LINE BETWEEN –LOVE AND HATE –JOY AND MISERY,

STUDY EVERYTHING and <u>MASTER</u> – Friction, sound, gravity, lines, water and energy 3, 6, 9 and 3669

Minutes to explain 1 - 4 to 5 shortly before the 24th hour go to 4, you got 4'

45° 50th connect the dots – look to where the other stars are even a slight variations (means disaccord) in universe (6/3). Go to <u>4</u> point to the stars ask are you with or against me. **Look for blinks.** Look <u>4</u> dead in his or her eyes. State record. Make a record. Do not believe. Make him put his mark next to, above, and straight across a dotted like; his mark = X 1.) acknowledge

1.)   9 is the center of the universe, makes final decisions, to make those stars, as they are and will put them back if <u>4</u> turns around and put his back to 0.

2.)   <u>O</u> is nothing, who hates <u>4</u>, caused division with 4/(3) and the one who loves him like no other

3.)   Tell <u>4</u> to profess out his mouth, <u>3 times</u>, saying it louder and louder; shout to the Universe.

(division sign); the one who loves you the most and like no other has created a division -- opposites.

Part 10

The Reasons You Count Your Numbers

To Be Counted For – Guide On A Journey
–To Account For

5° 5th Degree of angular diameter (faint) – 3 stars circle triple star

One of many – yet perfectly designed by a master that was created, himself by a master of all masters, and the answer to the meaning of life is numbered according to an evolving light, axis, angles -- An invisible line, separating ⁄ (division sign) equivalent to the pictured division symbol is what this force put together to generate light. Took a circle separated them.

Journey of many masters (confirmed one)

Inner Core – is ticking on a clock – on various axles in a Universe that created you with a speed that is not counted yet you must be accounted for.

1.) Count your daily bread -look to the stars – check your numbers

2.) Move -act upon 1.) thoughts, 2.) sense with numbers tell you and 3.) look to the stars

3.) Acknowledge -- Instincts – What is within you

Know Thyself and Thy Enemy
Isaiah 46:9-10

1.) <u>Be who God meant you to be</u> and you will set the world on fire. <u>Flame of fire</u> Heb 1:7

2.) <u>Be against, never with adversaries of God.</u> Acts 5:29
Playing the lottery to get rich – I asked the higher force to instruct me on how to respond to people who expect me to play the lottery for financial gain – Answer: use 1 Timothy 6:5

I must withdraw myself from such obsession. (Of course money is not evil but godliness with contentment is great gain). Constant friction between men of depraved minds who are devoid of the truth. These men do (but you should not) regard godliness as a means of gain. Their intellects are discorded. They are blinded to all knowledge. Their minds and consciousness are defiled. Titus 1:15

They have imaged, silly myths but you have God. Titus 1:11. They will undermine your household by wrong teachings. 1 Timothy 4:7. They will oppose your children because they oppose the truth – verdict – destruction. They do not sleep. 2 Peter 2:3

No man can serve two masters for he will <u>hate one and love the other.</u> Mt. 6-24
Money is material. It is a substance, not an answer although it is often used as a solution depending on one's perspective. But God is never changing, he is superior, he is the answer = the solution. Follow this path, step 1, step 2 and step 3 and you will master the universe.

Slippery slope – slide into help, slicker spot.

The devil is chaos, confusion, manipulator of words, and thoughts. He is conceited and understands nothing. Instead he has an unhealthy interest in controversies and semantics, and constant friction. He will use God's words to destroy you. John 10:29.

The devil misuses numbers and destroys lives with lottery schemes by distorting the meaning of numbers.

HOW TO FIGHT
(DESTROY YOUR ENEMIES)

1.) <u>First, recognize you need the force to assist you</u>
2.) <u>Outsmart them -- be one step ahead of them</u>
3.) <u>Only answer what you are forced to respond to</u>
   <u>because they will use your words against you</u>

   <u>ANYTHING YOU SAY WILL BE HELD AGAINST YOU</u>
   a.) You cannot afford to misunderstand the question
   b.) You cannot afford to forget the answer

4.) <u>REMEMBER – Anyone engaged in these tactics ARE</u>
   <u>YOUR ENEMY - never a friend</u>

   a.) Do not let them touch you
   b.) Do not respond to them with opinions only facts
      (reflect intellect)

5.) <u>When they realize they cannot defeat you they will</u>

   a.) Profess they are superior and claim you are inferior
   b.) Insult your accomplishments yet they cannot
      compare
   c.) Attempt this to cause you to become bewildered
   d.) Cause you to become defensive – do not defend;
      present i.) your greatness, ii. intellect, character,
      iii. Get witnesses to vouch for you
   e.) When they attempt to cause you to become angry
      do not get off track; i.) use physical evidence and
      ii.) address them directly

6.) <u>Speak out loud to the force wait for answers so you can</u>
   <u>look right through their tactics</u>

Slippery slope – slide into help, slicker spot.

The devil is chaos, confusion, manipulator of words, and thoughts. He is conceited and understands nothing. Instead he has an unhealthy interest in controversies and semantics, and constant friction. He will use God's words to destroy you. John 10:29.

The devil misuses numbers and destroys lives with lottery schemes by distorting the meaning of numbers.

HOW TO FIGHT
(DESTROY YOUR ENEMIES)

1.) <u>First, recognize you need the force to assist you</u>
2.) <u>Outsmart them -- be one step ahead of them</u>
3.) <u>Only answer what you are forced to respond to</u>
   <u>because they will use your words against you</u>

   ANYTHING YOU SAY WILL BE HELD AGAINST YOU
   a.) You cannot afford to misunderstand the question
   b.) You cannot afford to forget the answer

4.) <u>REMEMBER – Anyone engaged in these tactics ARE</u>
   <u>YOUR ENEMY - never a friend</u>

   a.) Do not let them touch you
   b.) Do not respond to them with opinions only facts
      (reflect intellect)

5.) <u>When they realize they cannot defeat you they will</u>

   a.) Profess they are superior and claim you are inferior
   b.) Insult your accomplishments yet they cannot
      compare
   c.) Attempt this to cause you to become bewildered
   d.) Cause you to become defensive – do not defend;
      present i.) your greatness, ii. intellect, character,
      iii. Get witnesses to vouch for you
   e.) When they attempt to cause you to become angry
      do not get off track; i.) use physical evidence and
      ii.) address them directly

6.) <u>Speak out loud to the force wait for answers so you can</u>
   <u>look right through their tactics</u>

SCRIPTURES – HIDDEN, LOST MEMORY
Knowledge of Science and Language

Crescent – star with sword overhead, add a sword on upper part (stop knowledge of science/figures of speech); step forward- what will you do to help the force

Free Masons – (56) signers of the Declaration of Independence (9) were free masons – Duty to hide secrets Secrets known by the founding fathers. They know your history but you do not, while they master it.

Muslim sons, Master Shriners – study 37 years

Shriners – you must be a master in good standing

Ancient, Arabic order of the noble of the Mystic Shrine – sacred in tomb – sacred placed, associated

Temple/Mosque name after Mecca, Medina, Syria, Anouk
All part of the Muslim work – Arabic in name
Social, political, economic name in same – noble status in society

King Solomon's Temple

Who is the saint embodied in the Shrine? The holy person whose bones are in the shrine? Bones connected to originator, with him are the architects of the universe and all this is wisdom.

You are the direct descendants of God himself, the originator of the heaven and the earth -- Kalifa of God himself.

UNDERSTAND WHO YOU ARE

KNOW THEYSELF - KNOW THY ENEMY

How – What – When – Where – Why

1.) Have the ability to look at a problem without detail and still find the solution

2.) You must know even though they fail to understand you, you are a person of principles; not of the secular world but of spiritual intellect

3.) Wants to dummy you down; when you are superior = of royalty but have no crown they can view

4.) They are tricksters.

They will:

a.) Manipulate your thoughts

b.) Devalue your intellect

c.) Lie constantly

d.) Refuse to acknowledge, admit what they are doing is wrong (but want you to work hard, while they sit on their buttocks and laugh)

e.) Blame you for their faults, evil doing

f.) They hate you and are waiting for any minor slip up

g.) Will use your words against you even if they know it was a misstatement

i. You have to be perfect, invoke the power of the force
ii. You have to outsmart them; you are the master they are the flock and/or O's children (O's seeds)
iii. Be one step ahead of them at all times
iv. Never think the game will be fair.

Make A Plan – Outline, Graph, Look At All Angles